Fawn and the Mysterious Trickster

WRITTEN BY
LAURA DRISCOLL

ILLUSTRATED BY
BARBARA NELSON

& THE DISNEY STORYBOOK ARTISTS

A STEPPING STONE BOOK™
RANDOM HOUSE 🏠 NEW YORK

Library of Congress Cataloging-in-Publication Data

Driscoll, Laura.

Fawn and the mysterious trickster / written by Laura Driscoll ; illustrated by Barbara Nelson and the Disney Storybook Artists.

p. cm.

"A Stepping Stone book."

SUMMARY: Fawn and her best friend, fellow animal-talent fairy Beck, get into an all-out pranking battle before realizing that someone else may be getting in on the fun.

ISBN 978-0-7364-2507-0 (pbk.)

[1. Tricks—Fiction. 2. Dreams—Fiction. 3. Fairies—Fiction.] I. Nelson, Barbara, ill. II. Disney Storybook Artists. III. Title.

PZ7.D79Faw 2008

[Fic]—dc22   2007048210

www.randomhouse.com/kids/disney

Printed in the United States of America

10 9 8 7 6 5 4 3 2 1

All About Fairies

IF YOU HEAD toward the second star on your right and fly straight on till morning, you'll come to Never Land, a magical island where mermaids play and children never grow up.

When you arrive, you might hear something like the tinkling of little bells. Follow that sound and you'll find Pixie Hollow, the secret heart of Never Land.

A great old maple tree grows in Pixie Hollow, and in it live hundreds of fairies and sparrow men. Some of them can do water magic, others can fly like the wind, and still others can speak to animals. You see, Pixie Hollow is the Never fairies' kingdom, and each fairy who lives there has a special, extraordinary talent.

Not far from the Home Tree, nestled in the branches of a hawthorn, is Mother Dove, the most magical creature of all. She sits on her egg, watching over the fairies, who in turn watch over her. For as long as Mother Dove's egg stays well and whole, no one in Never Land will ever grow old.

Once, Mother Dove's egg *was* broken. But we are not telling the story of the egg here. Now it is time for Fawn's tale. . . .

Fawn
and the
Mysterious
Trickster

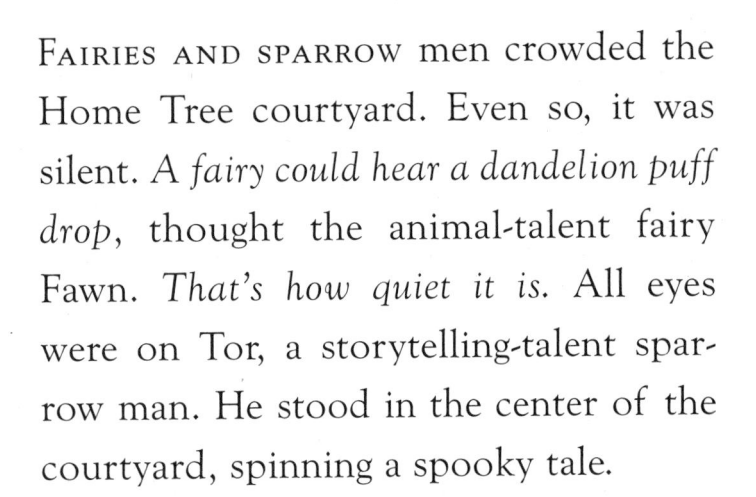

FAIRIES AND SPARROW men crowded the
Home Tree courtyard. Even so, it was
silent. *A fairy could hear a dandelion puff
drop*, thought the animal-talent fairy
Fawn. *That's how quiet it is.* All eyes
were on Tor, a storytelling-talent sparrow man. He stood in the center of the
courtyard, spinning a spooky tale.

It was just after dinner on Harvest Moon Night. After dinner was when the storytelling talents wove their tales. And on Harvest Moon Night, they told only spooky tales. The storytellers took turns trying to outdo one another.

The fairies had already heard Pip's tale of the giant ladybug. Next had come Merk's mystery about the wailing wind. But only now, during Tor's tale, did Fawn's friend Beck reach for her arm and hold it tight.

"Isn't this great?" whispered Beck, who was also an animal-talent fairy. Her eyes were wide, and she wore a huge grin. She was enjoying Tor's spine-tingling tale as much as Fawn was.

Fawn nodded. "This is the most

scared I've been in a long time!" she whispered gleefully. She wiggled in her seat and tapped her foot on the ground. She couldn't wait to hear what came next!

Tor was just getting to the scariest part of his story. "*Thump, scratch. Thump, scratch.* The mysterious noise grew louder and louder," he said. "The fairy backed away from the closed door. It was here, she realized. It was on the other side of the door. She stood frozen to the spot. The doorknob turned! With a long, low creak, the door . . . slowly . . . swung . . . open. Standing there in the shadowy darkness was—"

Pop! Crack! Boom! Three loud noises rang through the courtyard. All around the circle, fairies jumped—including Fawn. Bursts of bright red light filled the sky overhead. They formed the image of a hideous creature! It had the head of an eagle, its hooked beak open and screeching. The creature's springy legs and oversized feet looked like a hare's. A long, spiked dragon tail dragged behind it.

Some fairies gasped. Others cried out. But Fawn grinned. She figured Tor had set it all up. Fawn was a prankster herself, and she knew a good prank when she saw one.

The bursts of red light faded to black. For several breathless moments, no one moved.

Finally, Rani, a water-talent fairy,

broke the silence. "Tor, you really scared me!" she cried.

"Me too!" said Lily, a garden-talent fairy, peeking out from behind a toad-stool.

"That was the idea!" Tor said with a smile.

Slowly, the looks of fright became smiles of relief. Someone giggled. Then a wave of laughter swept around the courtyard.

Beck was laughing, too. She finally let go of Fawn's arm. Fawn had barely noticed Beck squeezing it all through the story's end. But now Fawn felt her hand tingling.

"That's some grip you've got there," she told Beck.

The stories were over. It was late. Fairies left the courtyard in twos and threes, flying slowly to the Home Tree. Fawn and Beck joined the others.

"Tor's story was the spookiest. Don't you think?" Beck asked Fawn.

"Yes!" Fawn agreed. She circled Beck, zipping around to fly on her left, then her right, then her left again. Fawn found it hard to stay in one place for more than a second. When she was excited, she could make other fairies dizzy!

"Tor's was definitely the best story," Fawn went on. "The prank at the end is what really made it scary!"

Beck nodded as they flew into the Home Tree lobby. "If only Harvest Moon Night came more often. Oh, well.

There's always next year!" she said with a sigh. "Or maybe what we need is . . ." Her voice trailed off. She stopped and stared off into the distance.

Fawn followed her gaze. "What? What do we need?" she asked.

"Huh?" Beck replied, snapping out of it.

"You said, 'What we need is . . .'?"

"Oh." Beck waved her hand. "Never mind. I mean, I forget. I mean . . ." She paused. Then she yawned a big yawn. A *very* big yawn. "Well, I'm off to bed," she announced. "See you later—I mean, tomorrow."

"Okay, Beck," said Fawn. "Good night. Don't let the bedbugs bite!" That was a joke. Fawn giggled. As animal talents, both she and Beck knew that bedbugs never bit fairies.

Fawn watched Beck fly up the stairs toward her room. Was it only her imagination, or was Beck acting funny all of a sudden? Just then, Tinker Bell and Rani zipped by.

"Wait up!" Fawn called after them, forgetting about Beck. "Wasn't Tor's story the best?" She flew circles around them as they headed into the tearoom for a late-night snack.

Two tea cakes later, Fawn flew up to her room. As she closed the door behind her, she sighed. She was sorry that the spooky storytelling was over.

Maybe I can get Tor to tell another spooky tale tomorrow night, she thought.

She dove onto her bed. She tugged off one boot and dropped it. It hit the floor with a thump.

Maybe he'll let me come up with a prank for the end, she thought.

Fawn dropped the other boot. *Thump.*

She lay back on her bed. *It's fun being scared. But it's even more fun to do the scaring!* she decided.

Thump. Fawn jumped. Had she just heard a third boot drop? Of course not. She only had two boots.

She peeked over the side of her bed.

Thump. The noise came again. But now it sounded like it was coming from the closet. But what was making it? Fawn flew off her bed. She was halfway to the closet when she heard it again. Only this time, it was more of a . . .

Thump, scratch.

Why, that sounded a bit like . . .

Thump, scratch.

It sounded strangely like . . .

Thump, scratch.

Like the sound from Tor's story!

In spite of herself, Fawn froze. "It's just a noise," she said out loud. "A spooky noise. A very, very spooky noise."

Fawn gave herself a little shake. Anything could be making that noise. An animal friend, for instance, like a cricket or a moth. Fawn flew closer to the closet door.

But . . . wait a second! Were her eyes

playing a trick? Or . . . had the doorknob just turned?

Great greedy groundhogs! It had! The doorknob was turning! Fawn watched it, frozen in horror. Now she knew it couldn't be an animal friend. She didn't know any animal that could turn a doorknob. Fawn backed away.

With a long, low creak, the door slowly swung open.

2

STANDING THERE IN the shadowy darkness was . . .

"Beck!" Fawn cried—or tried to. It came out a squeak. Fawn realized she'd been holding her breath.

"Boo!" shouted Beck. She flew to Fawn's side. "Did I scare you?" she asked hopefully.

"You scared the pixie dust off me!" Fawn replied. Then it dawned on her. "Wait. You were *trying* to scare me?"

Beck nodded. She flashed a proud smile. "Of course! Tor's story gave me the idea. So . . ."

Fawn sprang into the air. Her mind was racing. She was putting it all together.

"Is that what you were thinking about just before we said good night?" she asked Beck.

Beck laughed. Then she stopped laughing as something seemed to occur to her. "You aren't . . . *mad*, are you, Fawn?" she asked, looking worried.

Fawn thought it over. The flustered, spooked feeling was fading away. In its place was something else. It definitely wasn't anger. It was . . . pride!

"Mad?" Fawn replied, and a smile spread across her face. "No way! That was so great!" She threw an arm around Beck's shoulders.

Fawn had known Beck for years and years, and she thought she knew her friend better than anyone. But now Beck had really surprised her. "I didn't know you had it in you, Beck! You definitely got me good!"

Beck beamed. "Really? I wasn't sure I'd be able to prank the pranking queen."

Fawn's glow flared with delight. But she waved off the praise. "Don't be silly," she said. "I couldn't have done it better myself."

Hmm . . . Or could I? she wondered.

After all, a true prankster couldn't let a prank go unanswered, could she?

Three days later, Fawn woke at first light.

Quickly, she pulled off her pajamas and put on a pair of soft corn-husk pajamas that looked just like the ones Beck wore. Next, she pinned up her long braid. She tucked her dark hair under a corn-husk sleeping cap—just like Beck's. Lastly, she grabbed the copper-colored curtain fringe she had borrowed from the decoration talents. She carefully pinned it to the front of the cap.

Fawn had been planning this for days. She didn't know if she could fool Beck. But if she did, it would be the best prank she'd ever pulled.

Fawn flew to the mirror and studied her reflection. Her disguise wasn't perfect. For one thing, she couldn't make her brown eyes blue, like Beck's. Even so, Fawn was hoping she could fool one very sleepy fairy.

Fawn flew out of her room. She zipped down the corridor to Beck's room and pressed her ear to the door. All was silent. Then, slowly, Fawn pushed the door open and peeked inside.

Beck was in her leafy loft bed, still sound asleep. Fawn slipped inside the room, closing the door quietly behind her. She tried extra hard to move without making a noise. She flew across the room and dove behind Beck's dressing table.

Now came the last part. Fawn reached for the back of the sunflower mirror that sat atop the dressing table. She pulled out the tacks that held the mirror to its frame. She leaned the mirror against the back of the table and put the empty frame back in place.

Fawn heard Beck stir in her sleep. She peeked around the side of the dressing table. Beck tossed, then turned. She yawned. She propped herself up on her elbow. Then, slowly, with great effort, Beck dragged her feet over the side of the bed. For a second Fawn thought she had fallen asleep sitting up. But finally Beck got up and flew sleepily toward her dressing table.

This is it! thought Fawn. Her timing needed to be perfect. She strained to hear the flutter of Beck's wings as she got closer. When the moment was right, Fawn put on her best sleepy face. Beck sat down in her dressing table chair.

Framed in Beck's sunflower mirror was Fawn—looking just like Beck!

Beck's half-open eyes skimmed over the mirror. She fumbled with a pine-needle comb on the tabletop. Fawn made the same motion. She copied Beck perfectly. Then Beck looked into the mirror. Fawn stared sleepily back at her. Beck rubbed her eyes. Fawn rubbed her own. Beck yawned, and so did Fawn. Beck scratched her tummy. Fawn did, too.

Now let's see if she's paying attention, thought Fawn. As Beck was about to look away, Fawn winked.

Beck did a double take. She stared at Fawn. *Did I just see what I think I saw?* her face seemed to say. Fawn made her face say it, too. Beck shook her head,

then stretched. Fawn did the same. Beck leaned to one side. Fawn leaned to the opposite side. Beck noticed—and sat bolt upright. So did Fawn. Beck stared at the mirror warily. Fawn stared back. Beck stretched again, leaning to her right and watching her reflection. Fawn copied her. Then Fawn stuck out her tongue.

Startled, Beck covered her face with her hands. Fawn did, too, though she peeked through her fingers to see Beck's next move. Slowly, Beck lowered her hands. So did Fawn. Beck leaned closer to the mirror. Fawn leaned forward, too. There was no more than a gnat's length between the two fairies' noses. Fawn knew she wouldn't be able to fool Beck much longer.

In the blink of an eye, Fawn reached through the mirror frame . . . and tweaked Beck's nose!

"Iiieeee!" Beck screeched.

3

"WHAT . . . ? WHO . . . ? HOW . . . ?" Beck stammered. She stared wide-eyed at the face in her mirror.

Fawn pulled off her disguise. She explained the whole prank to Beck. Before long, Beck was laughing.

"That was amazing," Beck said. She threw up her hands in surrender. "I give up. I think you've proved who's the best prankster."

If Fawn hadn't known Beck so well, she might have missed the twinkle in her friend's eye. But she knew she hadn't heard the last from Beck!

At first, Fawn was on pins and needles waiting for the next prank. Every time she had a meal in the tearoom, she checked her chair before she sat down. When it was bedtime, she looked under her pillow before lying down. But days passed, and nothing happened.

Maybe Beck had given up after all! Fawn was a little disappointed in her friend. She'd thought Beck had more spunk than that.

One evening, just after dinner, Fawn

set out for the dairy barn. Every few days, she liked to check in on the dairy mice. Often she wound up visiting them late into the night.

Fawn made her way slowly to the barn. She would have flown faster, but she was weighed down by the sack of alfalfa seed she had brought as a treat for the mice.

Night had fallen by the time Fawn slid the barn door open and flew inside.

"Anyone here?" she squeaked in Mouse language into the dimly lit room.

The dairy mice squeaked a greeting back. Mice resting on their grassy beds came over to her. Mice snacking at their troughs left their food. Fawn was quickly surrounded by four-legged friends.

She passed out the alfalfa seed and gossiped with the mice as they snacked. Squeaking in Mouse was hard on a fairy's throat. Fawn was often hoarse the morning after a visit to the barn. But she didn't give that a second thought. She was having too much fun catching up with her friends.

Fawn had been talking for quite a while when she saw two shadows—a mouse's and her own—on the wall of the barn. Funny, she hadn't noticed them before. But she shrugged it off and went back to chatting.

But then a movement on the wall caught her eye. She glanced over. What was making that strange shadow? It wasn't a mouse shadow. Fawn knew that for sure. Whatever it belonged to had a giant head!

As Fawn watched, the shadow raised two enormous arms. Its long fingers were outstretched like claws! The huge shadow was three times the size of Fawn's—and only inches away! Whatever it was, it was right behind her!

Fawn wheeled around. But she didn't see any monster. She couldn't see anything! Her eyes, which had adjusted to the faint light of the barn, squinted into a blinding light.

All of a sudden, the bright light dimmed. Fawn blinked several times.

There was Beck, her wings tucked in. She had been playing the part of the giant, hulking shadow monster. Behind

her was Fira, a light-talent fairy. They were both giggling over their shadow trick.

Fawn took a deep breath. She groaned. "Beck! You got me again!" She felt like kicking herself for being fooled. She had been ready—and she'd gotten tricked anyway!

Still, Fawn was always a good sport. She congratulated Beck and Fira on their fine—and frightening—prank.

But of course, Fawn wasn't about to be outdone.

Over the next few days, the pranks came fast and furious. Beck slyly tied a tiny wooden whistle to Fawn's wing so that a mysterious sound followed Fawn around all day. Then Fawn replaced

Beck's shampoo with maple syrup. Beck's hair stood straight up for two days and five washings! Beck sprinkled fairy dust onto Fawn's breakfast roll so that it floated away before Fawn could eat it. Fawn replaced Beck's favorite clothes with bigger and bigger sizes to make her think she was shrinking.

One night, Beck stuffed two dozen maple seedpods into Fawn's closet. They rained down on Fawn when she went to get dressed the next morning.

As she stood in a mound of seedpods, Fawn couldn't help admiring Beck's creativity. "Pretty good, Beck," she said. "But you haven't seen my best pranks yet!"

All day long, Fawn plotted. At breakfast, she pretended to listen while Beck shared the details of her seedpod prank with the rest of the animal-talent table. But inside, Fawn was scheming.

Fawn plotted while visiting friends. She looked for ideas first in Rosetta's garden and then in Tink's workshop. She didn't find any.

Fawn was still plotting at bedtime. She lay under her covers, thinking. She wanted her next prank to be a really good one. She wanted it to be something new—something different. But nothing was coming to her!

She drifted off to sleep, still thinking about pranks.

That night, Fawn dreamed that she and Beck were on a beach. They stood side by side at the water's edge. Beck filled an acorn cup with seawater. She emptied it into a shell bucket at Fawn's feet. Beck turned to fill the cup again. When Beck wasn't looking, Fawn dumped the bucket out onto the sand. She put it down before Beck turned around. Beck refilled the bucket. Fawn dumped it out again. Beck kept filling. Fawn kept secretly emptying—turning the bucket over, over, over. Fawn-in-the-dream giggled. At this rate, Beck would never fill the bucket!

Fawn awoke to sunlight on her pillow. Bits of the dream were still floating around in her mind.

"Wow!" she said to herself. "I'm even pranking in my sleep!"

Then she groaned. She *still* didn't have a good idea. If only her silly dream prank had been good enough to use in real life!

4

FAWN'S BEDROOM DOOR burst open. There stood Beck, hands planted on her hips.

"Okay," she said. "I have *no* idea how you did it—and without waking me up!"

"Huh?" Fawn said, sitting up in bed.

"When did you do it?" Beck went

on. "Last night after I went to sleep?" She flew to Fawn's bed and plopped down next to her. "Or did you get up early this morning? I wish I could have seen my own face," Beck said, laughing. "When I woke up and looked around, I couldn't figure out what was going on. With everything upside down, I felt like *I* was upside down!"

Fawn pinched herself hard. "Ow!" she cried. "Yep, I'm awake. But I still don't know what you're talking about."

"Don't be silly!" Beck said. "You know, the prank. My stuff . . . my room . . . turned upside down!"

"What?" Fawn cried. She had to see this for herself. She pulled on her tunic and pumpkin-colored leggings. Then she

Fawn smiled, then giggled. "It is funny," she agreed. "I only wish *I* had thought of it!"

Beck did a double take. "What?"

"I didn't do it!" Fawn insisted. "Really!" Beck still didn't believe her—Fawn could tell by the look on her face. There was only one way to convince her. "Beck, I swear! I swear on Mother Dove's egg. It wasn't me."

Beck looked Fawn in the eye. Swearing on Mother Dove's egg was the most solemn swear a Never fairy could make.

Beck's brow wrinkled. She looked around her. She seemed to be seeing the prank in a whole new way. "But Fawn," she said, "if *you* didn't do it . . ."

Fawn nodded. "Who did?"

Fawn and Beck thought about it until it was time for breakfast. They were still puzzling over it as they flew down to the tearoom.

"I bet it was a friend of ours," Beck was saying. "Someone who knows what we've been up to."

At that moment, the garden-talent fairy Rosetta flew into the tearoom. She heard Beck and came over. "Just what *have* you two been up to?" she asked playfully. "More pranks?"

Fawn described Beck's upside-down room to Rosetta. "But I didn't do it," Fawn said. "It was a mystery mischief-maker! A secret spooker! Another fairy is getting in on our pranking fun." She looked at Rosetta. "You don't know anything about it, do you?"

"Nope!" was all Rosetta said in reply. Then she flew off to the garden-talent table.

Beck leaned close to Fawn. "She doesn't seem like the most likely culprit," Beck pointed out. "Turning things upside down is hard work. She wouldn't want to mess up her hair."

"But you know what they say," Fawn replied. "Sometimes it's the fairy you *don't* suspect!"

Beck nodded thoughtfully.

The two fairies found seats together at the animal-talent table. Fawn was reaching for a slice of lemon poppy-seed cake when Tinker Bell flew by.

"Fawn, Beck," Tink called. "What's new with the pranking?"

Fawn spun around in her seat. "Why do you ask?" she replied. She fixed Tink with a questioning stare.

But Tink didn't seem to notice. She gave them a little wave and flew on to the pots-and-pans-talent table.

"Now, Tink . . . ," Fawn said to Beck. "She's not one to shy away from mischief. She might have done it!"

Fawn and Beck had a delicious breakfast of lemon poppy-seed cake and fresh-squeezed berry juice, but Fawn's thoughts were never far from Beck's prankster.

As they were leaving the tearoom, Fira flew in. "Fly with you, Beck," she called, using the traditional fairy greeting. She winked at Fawn as she passed by them.

Fawn stopped in midair and turned. "Wait!" she called after Fira.

"What?" Fira said, flying backward.

"You winked at me!" Fawn said. "Why?"

Fira gave Fawn a funny look. "Well, you know. The prank the other day. In the barn. I helped Beck trick you," she reminded Fawn. "I hope there are no hard feelings."

Beck studied Fira's face carefully. "Is that all?"

Fira nodded. "What else would there be?" she asked. She seemed completely confused.

"You tell us!" Fawn said.

For a second, Fira was at a loss for words. Then she laughed. "You two are funny," she said, and flew on.

Fawn turned to Beck. "I've got it!" she exclaimed. "Fira had fun pranking *me*. So she decided to prank you, too! You know, just to be fair!"

Beck looked doubtful. "But she really didn't seem to know anything about it."

Fawn had to admit Beck was right. Fira was probably innocent.

For the rest of the day, the two fairies were on the lookout for suspects. Was it Terence, a fairy-dust talent? He and Tink kept whispering to each other during the big game of acorn ball.

Or was it Terra or Finn, two other animal talents? They *had* been giggling a lot at dinner.

That evening in Fawn's room, Fawn and Beck wrote down all their suspects on a leaf. It was a long list. In fact, just about everyone was a suspect! But they had no real leads.

Fawn flew around the room. She scratched her head and tried to puzzle it out.

Beck was sitting on Fawn's bed. She let out a big sigh. "I guess we aren't any closer to figuring out who our mystery prankster is," she said.

They were both silent. The wind picked up outside the Home Tree. It whistled eerily through the hollow spaces of the great old maple. Suddenly, Fawn stopped and stared at Beck. Her eyes widened.

"What if our prankster *isn't* a fairy?" she said.

Beck's brow wrinkled. "What do you mean?" she asked.

"Maybe it's not a fairy! Not a sparrow

man! Not even . . . of this world!" Fawn cried. She landed next to Beck. "What if our prankster is . . . a *ghost?*"

Outside the window, lightning flashed. A second later, a clap of thunder boomed.

Both fairies jumped.

"Beck," said Fawn, "what if the Home Tree is haunted?"

5

THAT NIGHT, FAWN slept fitfully. She dreamed of ghosts floating through the halls of the Home Tree.

The next morning, just like every morning, Fawn woke up and threw her legs over the side of her bed. Just like every morning, her feet felt around for her slippers. Just like every morning, her feet found the slippers lined up neatly next to her bed.

But this morning, *unlike* every morning, her feet came down on the slippers with a squishy *splat*.

With a sinking feeling, Fawn looked down. Her slippers were covered with a shiny green goo!

"Eewwww!" Fawn cried, wincing. Her feet had goo all over them! She looked at them more closely. "What in Never Land is this stuff?" She glanced around for something to wipe her feet with. That was when she noticed:

There was green goo all over her mirror!

Fawn flew out of bed. Her dresser was covered in goo, too. Her toadstool night table, the foot of her bed—lots of things had little splatters or smears or glops of it. Blobs of green goo dotted her floor. They seemed to form a little trail leading toward the door.

Just as Fawn was getting dressed, there was a knock. Beck rushed in.

"I've been slimed!" she cried. Then she noticed Fawn's mirror. "Oh! You've been slimed, too!"

"What?" Fawn exclaimed. "*You've* been slimed? With this stuff?"

"Well, my room has," Beck replied. "Come look."

Fawn followed Beck down the corridor. Sure enough, when they reached Beck's room, Fawn saw a slimy mess.

Beck studied a glob of slime on her doorknob. "What *is* it?"

"I don't know," said Fawn. More slime on the floor outside Beck's door caught her eye. "But there's some out here!" Fawn zipped farther down the corridor. "And over here! And down there, too!" She looked back at Beck. "Let's see where it leads!" Fawn cried.

Beck hesitated. "Should we?" she said. "We don't know what this stuff is. Or why it's here. Or who—or what— might have left it behind."

Fawn rubbed her hands excitedly. "You mean like a ghost?" she asked.

"Yes," Beck replied. "Or a giant fairy-eating snail or something!"

"Oooo, even better!" exclaimed Fawn. She grabbed Beck's hand. "Come on! Let's go!"

Leading the way, Fawn followed the trail of slime. It ran down the stairs to the lobby. From there, it wandered into the tearoom.

Some early-rising fairies already were there having breakfast. Fawn and Beck weaved around the tables. They dodged kitchen-talent fairies carrying baskets of muffins. No one else seemed to notice the slime. It blended in well with the tearoom's fresh flower carpet. But Fawn and Beck knew what they were looking for.

They kept their eyes on the trail. It led them through the swinging door of the kitchen. Inside, the kitchen talents were busily preparing breakfast. Some stirred pots on the stove. Others washed dishes. One fairy carried a pan to the top shelf of the floor-to-ceiling pot rack. Fawn and Beck zigged and zagged around them—one eye on the kitchen traffic and one eye on the slime.

Then, in the pantry, the trail ended. Fawn and Beck stopped. They hovered and looked all around. But there was no more slime to be seen.

"That's it?" said Beck, looking down. "That's the end?"

"I don't think so," Fawn replied. "I think *this* is the end." She pointed to the cupboard in front of them. "I'll bet that whatever made the slime is *inside this cupboard.*"

Beck drew back. Fawn held her breath. She flung open the cupboard doors. But all she found were jars, tins, canisters—the usual pantry stuff.

Fawn let out a sigh of relief . . . and disappointment. But then—

"Wait!" she cried. "This jar . . ." She picked up a jar from a shelf. It was missing its lid. A teaspoon was sticking out. "It's dripping with slime!" Fawn examined the jar more closely. "It's *filled* with slime! No, not slime. It's . . ."

"What? What?" Beck cried.

Fawn said nothing. Instead, she scooped up some slime with her finger. Then, with a wink at Beck, *she ate it!*

"Fawn! No!" Beck grabbed the slimy jar out of her friend's hand. She stared wide-eyed at Fawn. "What are you doing?"

Fawn just smiled.

Beck looked down at the jar. Its label was staring her in the face.

Beck's jaw dropped. "*Kiwifruit jam?*" she exclaimed in disbelief.

Fawn started to laugh. She laughed so hard she snorted. "Someone *really* got us, Beck," she said between guffaws.

Before long, Beck was doubled over laughing, too. A couple of kitchen talents peeked into the pantry. They threw Fawn and Beck questioning looks, but the two fairies were laughing too hard to explain anything.

Finally, the laughing fit tapered off. Fawn took deep breaths. She held the laughing cramp in her side.

"Well, at least we know one thing for sure," Beck said.

"What?" Fawn asked.

"This was the work of our mystery prankster," said Beck. "And it's *definitely* a fairy or a sparrow man."

Fawn thought it over for a second. "How do you know?" she asked.

"Think about it," said Beck. "What

6

It took Fawn and Beck hours to clean up all the green jam. And Fawn still felt sticky between her toes. But at least she and Beck were in it together. Fawn listened to Beck fluffing her pillows in the semidarkness. Beck was settling into a little bed she and Fawn had made in Fawn's room. She hadn't wanted to sleep alone in her room, not after two nights in a row of unexplained mischief.

"We'll have a sleepover!" Fawn had suggested that afternoon. "It'll be fun." She'd flown excitedly around Beck. "Maybe we'll set a trap for our mystery prankster!"

And so they had. Across Fawn's doorway, they had tacked a superfine spiderweb. The web was nearly invisible. Then they had tied a row of bells along its edges. They were the tiniest handbells the music-talent fairies had—the ones with the highest pitch.

They had set up another similar trap across Fawn's open window.

As she snuggled in for the night, Fawn felt confident. "No one is getting in here without us knowing about it," she said.

"No *fairy*, you mean," Beck replied. Fawn could hear the smile in her voice. "Ghosts can float right through spider-webbing."

"True!" Fawn replied. "Well, then at least we'll know for sure. Did you tell our friends about the sleepover?"

"Yep," Beck said. "I dropped it into conversations all day long."

"Me too," Fawn said. "If someone wants to pull a prank, she'll know where to find us both! Then we'll find *her*—in the booby trap!" She rolled over. "Sleep well, Beck."

"Sleep well, Fawn," Beck replied.

But falling asleep wasn't easy. Fawn

found herself straining to hear every little nighttime noise. Her mind replayed the events of the day—slime tracking, slime cleaning, sleepover planning, and trap designing. She noticed a soft sound. It was Beck breathing, sound asleep. Fawn found herself breathing in the same rhythm—in, out, in, out, in . . .

The next thing she knew, a strange sound startled Fawn awake. She wasn't sure how long she had been sleeping. She wasn't even sure what kind of sound had woken her.

"Fawn, did you hear that?" asked Beck. She was sitting up on her pile of cushions.

"I heard something," Fawn replied. "What was it?"

There it was again. It was a creepy wail. Beck looked at Fawn with wide eyes.

"*That* was it," she said.

As animal talents, Fawn and Beck had heard plenty of strange noises. But this noise was different. This didn't seem like any animal sound—at least, not one Fawn had ever heard. This was eerie and unnatural. It was like a sound from another world.

"Come on! We've got to find out what's making it!" Fawn said. She leaped out of bed and flew to Beck's side. She grabbed Beck's hand to help her up. But Beck held back.

"We do?" Beck asked nervously. "Why?"

"Come on, Beck! Are you a fairy or a mouse?" Fawn asked.

"I've known a lot of very brave mice," Beck pointed out. "Remember Whiskers?"

"Good point," Fawn said. "So pretend you're Whiskers. Now, let's go! Quick! Before it stops!"

Fawn paused. "Where is it coming from, anyway?" Without thinking, she flung the door open and stuck her head out to listen.

"Fawn, wait!" Beck cried.

But it was too late.

BRRRRRRRRRIIIIIIIIIIIINNNG! Fawn's head got caught in the trap. All the tiny handbells rang loudly.

"Aaaah!" Fawn cried in alarm.

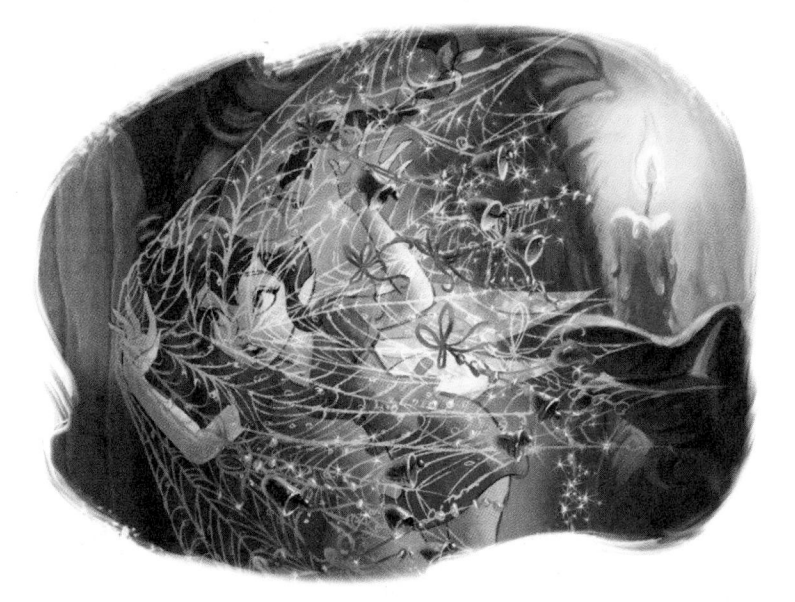

Beck cringed and covered her ears.

The spiderweb came loose from the doorframe. It stuck to Fawn's head and shoulders. As she struggled to get it off, the bells continued to ring. Finally, with Beck's help, Fawn removed the web. She dropped it on the floor.

"Now we know the trap works!"

said Fawn. Her heart was pounding.

They heard the wail again. "It's coming from outside the window," Fawn said. "But that's booby-trapped, too." She led the way into the corridor. "We'll go this way instead!"

Together Beck and Fawn flew down to the lobby. At the front door, they stopped. Slowly, they stuck their heads outside. They peered out at blackness. It was a cloudy night. No moon—nothing to see by.

Even so, Fawn flew out into the darkness. Beck followed.

"Beck! Look!" Fawn whispered. "Over there!" She pointed to a spot on a branch of the Home Tree. As they stared, something moved ever so slightly.

There was a faint rustling of leaves. A moment later, they heard the wail again.

Beck pointed just beyond the end of the branch. "Isn't that your window, Fawn?" she whispered.

Fawn nodded. "Whatever it is, it's sitting right outside my room!"

Just then, a dark shape darted from the leaves.

Fawn could barely make it out. It was about the size of a fairy, but she didn't see any wings. And yet it could fly! The thing hovered in the air, motionless as a statue. While Fawn watched, it moved to one side and hovered motionless again.

It let out a piercing wail that made Fawn's hair stand on end.

"What is it?" Beck whispered in Fawn's ear.

"I don't know. I can't make it out," Fawn whispered back. "But I know one thing."

"What?" said Beck.

Fawn swallowed hard. "That's no fairy."

7

THE MYSTERIOUS SHAPE disappeared behind another cluster of leaves.

"Let's get a closer look!" Fawn whispered.

They inched forward, moving as quietly as they could. Fawn strained to see. Over the rustling of leaves she noticed another sound—a pounding. It took her a moment to realize it was her heart beating.

Before they could reach the spot, the shape darted away. It moved almost too fast for Fawn to track it. The mysterious figure landed on a nearby branch. Another slight rustle of leaves gave it away. Again, Fawn and Beck inched toward it. And again, it darted to the next branch just as they got close.

On the third try, they closed in. They paused in front of the leaves shielding the mystery wailer. Fawn reached out and grasped a leaf stem. Slowly, slowly, she pulled the curtain of leaves aside.

A small, feathered head with a long, thin beak poked out at them.

"Twitter?" Beck cried in surprise.

Fawn was shocked speechless for several moments. She couldn't believe that the source of that awful wail was her and Beck's hummingbird friend.

Twitter and Beck had been close since Twitter was a chick. As long as

Beck had known him, Twitter had always been a little high-strung. He tended to get overexcited about the smallest things. When he did, he often came looking for Beck.

"Twitter," said Beck in Hummingbird, "what are you doing up at this time of night? And why are you making that awful noise? Are you all right?"

Unlike Beck, Fawn was still in prankster-hunting mode. She couldn't help eyeing Twitter suspiciously.

"Wait!" Fawn cried in Hummingbird. "I've got it now. *You're* the mystery prankster!"

Beck looked shocked. Twitter himself looked positively bewildered. "What p-p-prankster? N-n-no!" He flitted around excitedly as he twittered. He darted inches to the right and hovered. He darted inches to the left and hovered.

Fawn made other fairies dizzy, but Twitter made *Fawn* dizzy. She understood why she'd thought the dark shape was wingless. Twitter's wings flapped so fast she couldn't see them!

And sometimes Twitter's *brain* worked so fast his mouth had a hard time keeping up. "I j-j-just have a little c-c-cold," Twitter stuttered. "I couldn't sleep. I just d-d-didn't know what to do with myself. So I came out here to p-p-practice my new hummingbird song. Like this."

Twitter tipped his head back. Out came the noise that had woken Fawn and

Beck. Only, now it didn't sound much like a wail. It sounded like a humming-bird with a cold trying to sing.

"Aaaaaaaaoooooooooooooeeeeeeeee!" Twitter moaned.

Fawn's and Beck's eyes met. They couldn't help smiling. To think they had mistaken a singing bird for a wailing ghost!

Twitter stopped singing. "Do you like it?" he asked. "I made it up myself. I especially like the high part that goes like this. *Erreeeeeeeeeeeee!*"

Beck cleared her throat. "It's a very good song, Twitter. But you must be tired. Maybe you should try to get some sleep, and finish practicing your song in the morning."

The fairies flew Twitter back to his nest and tucked him in. Then they laughed over their silliness all the way back to the Home Tree.

"I think we're a little wound up over this ghost idea," Beck said.

"Yes," Fawn replied. "I guess we really let our imaginations run wild."

By the time they flew back into Fawn's room, they could barely keep their eyes open.

Fawn fell into her bed. There was nothing standing between her and sleep.

"*Ieee!*"

Fawn cringed in her sleep. She thought she heard seagulls. But why would there be seagulls in the Home Tree?

Fawn rolled over. She shielded her still-closed eyes from the morning sunshine. Her eyelids felt heavy. She struggled to get them open. But what she saw woke her up fast.

There weren't any seagulls—only Dulcie, a baking-talent fairy. She was looking down at Fawn, her eyes wide and her mouth open in surprise.

"Aaaah!" Fawn cried, startled.

Fawn looked over Dulcie's head. *That's funny,* she thought. *Who moved that pot rack from the kitchen to my room?*

Fawn sat bolt upright. *She* was in the kitchen. She looked down. This wasn't her bed—she'd been lying on a table.

This wasn't her blanket on top of her—it was a tablecloth.

Fawn knew she had fallen asleep in her bedroom. So how had she gotten down to the kitchen? There seemed to be only one explanation, and Fawn could hardly believe it.

The mystery prankster had *moved her as she slept*!

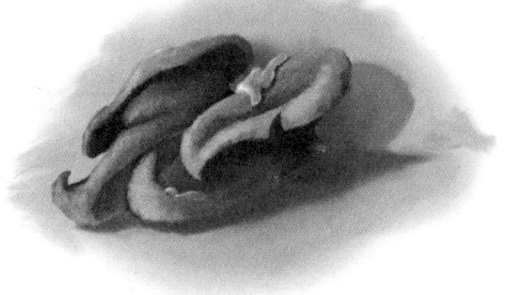

8

POOR DULCIE. HER glow was still trembling a little as she told Fawn how she had found her.

As everyone knew, Dulcie was the first baking talent in the kitchen each morning. She churned out a dozen batches of poppy puff rolls before the kitchen got too busy.

"I was going to get all my ingredients from the pantry," Dulcie told Fawn. "I came over to put them on this table. You were completely covered by the table-cloth." Dulcie held up Fawn's "blanket." "I didn't have any idea you were there until I moved it and . . . well, you can imagine my surprise!"

Fawn didn't have to imagine. She had seen—and heard—it for herself!

"But I don't understand," Dulcie went on. "You say someone moved you from your bed? While you slept? As a joke?" She crossed her arms. "It doesn't seem very funny to me."

Fawn put an arm around Dulcie. "Really? Because I think it's hilarious! And get this—a mystery prankster has gotten Beck and me before." She told Dulcie about Beck's upside-down room and the kiwifruit jam pranks. "See?" Fawn said. She pointed at her feet. "There's still some dried jam on my slippers."

Dulcie giggled. "That is kind of funny. But who do you think is behind it?" she asked.

"I have no idea!" Fawn exclaimed in frustration. Was the same prankster behind all the tricks, she wondered, or were there different ones? Or maybe it was a team of pranksters?

After she left the kitchen, Fawn raced upstairs to wake Beck. She had to tell her what had happened!

Fawn flew past her own door on her

way to Beck's before she remembered—
Beck was sleeping in Fawn's room. Fawn
backtracked and burst through the door.

"Beck! Beck!" she cried. "You've got
to hear this!" Fawn lifted the sheet that
Beck had pulled over her face while
she slept.

"Huh?" Beck grunted sleepily. But she woke up in a hurry when Fawn launched into her tale.

"The *kitchen*?" Beck repeated in disbelief after Fawn was done. "You mean someone moved you down there while you slept? Without even waking you up? How?"

"Well," Fawn said, "I *am* a very sound sleeper."

Beck snorted. "I know! Who's the one who always has to get you up for midnight visits with the bats? You could sleep through a jackrabbit migration."

Then Beck frowned. "But . . . how did the prankster even get in here?" she asked. "The place was booby-trapped."

Fawn shook her head. "Not quite.

Remember, we tripped the trap on the door last night?"

"Oh, right," Beck said. "When we came back to bed, we didn't set it up again."

"I guess the prankster came right in through the door," said Fawn. "Ooo! We were so close! If only we had reset the trap, we'd have caught the culprit!"

Fawn flew slowly to one side of the room while staring at the floor. Then she turned and flew slowly to the other side. Beck watched her. After crossing the room a dozen times, Fawn stopped.

"Okay. I say we go all out," Fawn said. "Tonight. We set up booby traps again, only this time, we set up more! And not just here, but all over the Home

Tree! We'll put one outside each fairy and sparrow man's door! Then, when the prankster comes out to start pranking, *boom!* We've got 'em!"

Fawn glanced at Beck for a reaction. Beck gave her a doubtful look.

"You're right, you're right." Fawn sighed. "That's a little crazy. Okay. How about this—we set a couple of traps in each main corridor. That's bound to catch anyone who's flying around and up to no good."

Now Beck looked more convinced. "Let's do it," she said. "There's just one thing. What if a fairy is just flying down to grab a snack or something? What if we catch someone who's not the prankster?"

Fawn waved the question away.

"We can worry about that when we catch someone!"

Getting the trap ready took most of the day. Fawn got rolls and rolls of spiderweb from the weaving talents. She was itching to tell them what it was for. But she knew she had to keep the plan a secret.

Fawn was already unrolling the webs in her room when Beck came in with the bells. As they tied the bells to the webs, they worked out the plan. They would wait to set up the traps until everyone was asleep. Otherwise, fairies would be tripping the traps left and right.

"And this time, I'm not going to sleep," said Fawn. "I want to stay alert— no mistakes like last time."

Beck wanted to stay up, too. "But if we're not going to sleep, what will we do?" she asked.

Fawn smiled. "We should find a good spot out in the hallway. Some-where we can see anyone coming. Then we'll hide . . . we'll watch . . . and we'll wait."

9

"Do YOU SEE anyone?" Beck whispered.

"No, no, not yet," Fawn whispered back.

The two fairies were squished into a tiny space behind a plant stand. The stand stood at a bend in the hallway where this branch of the Home Tree shot off in a different direction.

Beck peeked out from behind one side of the plant stand. Fawn peeked out the other side. By the faint light of the firefly lanterns on the wall, Beck could see the door of her room. And Fawn could see the door of her room. Together they could keep an eye on both corridors that led to their corner.

In each of the Home Tree's main corridors, they had set two traps. Fawn squinted, trying to make out the traps in her corridor. There was one about halfway down, and one at the far end. But it was too dark to see any of the superfine webs.

"Do you see anyone *now?*" Beck whispered.

"No," Fawn whispered. "No one."

Fawn and Beck sat pressed back to back. Fawn shifted slightly, trying to get more comfortable. There was little room to move. Fawn hated sitting still. This was practically torture!

Time inched by. Fawn stared down the corridor. She studied every detail. She noticed weird shadows under each lantern, and she tried to guess what was making them. An image of a scary face sprang into her mind. Fawn decided she didn't like that game.

She heard the trees outside rustle in the wind. A cold breeze ran down the corridor. Fawn shivered.

Crrrrrreeeeeeeeeak. The two fairies jumped at the noise. Fawn laughed nervously. "Just the Home Tree bending in the wind," she whispered.

They were both silent for several moments, listening. Then Beck whispered, "Fawn, what if . . . what if we don't catch anyone and we're still pranked?"

"What?" Fawn whispered. "You mean, what if someone gets by all our traps?" She couldn't see how. There were so many. They were everywhere. They were secret, and next to invisible. "If someone did that and still pranked us? Then I guess . . . that would *prove* that our prankster is . . . a ghost."

Out of the corner of her eye, Fawn saw something. A stone's throw away, a small, dark shape moved across the floor. It was coming toward Fawn!

"Aaaah!" Fawn cried, startling Beck behind her.

"What?" Beck cried, turning to see.

Fawn stammered, "It's a . . . a . . ."

The dark shape skittered away down the corridor. Fawn exhaled. It was just a beetle, passing through the Home Tree.

It took a while for Fawn's heart to

stop racing. Waiting for . . . *something* in the near-dark in the middle of the night was spookier than she had expected.

She took some deep breaths. She leaned her head against the plant stand. Behind her, Beck started humming very softly. Fawn guessed she was doing it out of nervousness. Or boredom. Either way, it was nice, and quiet enough that only she and Beck could hear.

Fawn listened to Beck's song. "Fairy Dust Melody"—that was what Beck was humming. The music talents had played it at the last Full Moon Dance.

Fawn smiled as she remembered. She hated the dressing-up part of twilight dances. But she loved the dancing part. She never understood why fairies like Rosetta bothered with delicate pine-needle-heeled slippers. Everyone just wound up kicking off their shoes when the music started!

Fawn closed her eyes just for a second. She could see the courtyard as it had looked that evening. The light-talent fairies had made lovely colored lanterns. The decoration talents had hung ribbon streamers from the low branches. The cooking and baking talents had filled tables with special treats. And, once the dance was in full swing, there had been all those fairies and sparrow men dancing. All the different colors of the fairies' dresses mingled together, swirling around, and around, and around. . . .

Just then, a loud ringing filled the hallway.

BRRRRRRRRRIIIIIIIIIIIINNNG!

The trap!

Fawn snapped awake. She scanned the dark corridor. "Who is it?" she cried. "Where are they? Beck? Beck?"

Beck was standing nearby. She stared at Fawn with wide eyes.

"Beck, why are you just standing there? The trap! It's been tripped!" said Fawn.

Beck said nothing.

"Beck, who's the prankster?" Fawn asked.

Beck opened her mouth to speak, then closed it again. She raised an arm slowly and pointed.

Fawn looked down. Wrapped all around her body were superfine spiderwebs tied with bells. Only then did she also notice that she wasn't crouched behind the plant stand. She was standing in the middle of the hallway. How had she gotten there? She had no memory of moving.

"Beck, I don't understand," Fawn said. "What's going on? Where's the mystery trickster?"

"Fawn," Beck said breathlessly, "the trickster is . . . *you!*"

10

"Yes, yes," Fawn replied impatiently. "I am a trickster. But who is *the* trickster? The *mystery* trickster!" She was trying to get airborne, but the spiderwebs kept her wings from moving freely. "Could you give me a hand with this?"

Beck stretched the sticky webs so that Fawn could wriggle out. "What *I* mean is that *you* are the mystery trickster!" Beck said.

Fawn couldn't believe what she was hearing. "That's ridiculous!" she replied. "Wouldn't I know if I were?"

Beck shook her head. "Not if you were sleeping."

Fawn stopped wriggling. "Sleeping?" she cried. "Sleeping while I turned your room upside down? Sleeping while I spread jam all over the Home Tree? Sleeping while I went downstairs to nap on a kitchen table?" She looked at Beck doubtfully. "Beck, come on. You've got to admit it sounds very unlikely."

Beck nodded. "I agree. It does," she said. "Does dancing in your sleep sound just as unlikely?"

"Yes," Fawn replied. "Why?"

"Because I just watched you dance in your sleep," Beck said. "You danced right into that booby trap."

It took a moment for that to sink in.

Beck went on. "Just now, before you tripped the trap, you got up from behind the plant stand. I asked what you were doing. But you didn't answer. Then you started twirling around the hallway." Beck closed her eyes and demonstrated.

"I called your name over and over. Your eyes were shut and you didn't seem to hear me. Before I knew it, you had danced right into the trap. And when the bells went off . . . you woke up." Beck stopped dancing and shrugged. "Fawn, I think you were *sleepflying!*"

Fawn was quiet. She was taking it all in. She wanted to laugh it off. But a voice inside was telling her that Beck was on to something. She *had* just been thinking—okay, dreaming—about the twilight dance. That would explain the dancing part of the sleepflight.

But what about the unexplained pranks?

Fawn thought back to the night Beck's room was turned upside down. "I had a dream the night of the first mystery prank," Fawn recalled. "I was turning a bucket of water over, again and again."

Beck thought about that. "Maybe you were acting that out in my room?" she suggested. "Did you have a dream the night of the jam prank?"

Fawn shook her head. "I don't remember one. But I *do* love kiwifruit jam," she said. "Maybe I was hungry for a midnight snack!"

Beck held up a finger. "And maybe you were going back for more the night you wound up on the kitchen table!"

Fawn shrugged. Who knew what a sleepflying fairy wanted or why she did it? But the sleepflying prankster theory was starting to add up.

"I think you might be right, Beck!" Fawn exclaimed. "I *am* the mystery prankster!" A huge grin spread slowly across her face. "And I'm such a good prankster, I can do it in my sleep!"

Beck crossed her arms. "No fair!" she cried. "I'm really going to have to watch out now. You're pranking day *and* night!"

Fawn still had trouble believing it. But she knew it had to be true. She and Beck had gotten so carried away with their pranking that it had taken over every part of their lives—even Fawn's sleep.

Suddenly, Fawn felt very tired. She yawned a huge yawn. She hadn't been sleeping well lately, and now she knew why. But she had a feeling that tonight she was going to sleep like a sloth. She didn't have to worry about ghosts or mystery pranksters anymore.

As Fawn went back to her own bed, she made a decision. She'd set up a booby trap in her door and one in her window every night before she went to bed. It would make her feel better. She didn't really want to be pranking other fairies in her sleep.

Of course, Fawn's pranking *days* weren't over.

The next morning, Fawn waved cheerfully at Beck as she flew into the tearoom for breakfast. "Fly with you, Beck!" Fawn said.

"Fly with you, Fawn!" replied Beck. She took the seat next to Fawn and reached for a platter of pancakes. "Up to any more midnight mystery pranks last night?" she asked.

"Not that I can remember!" Fawn replied.

Beck picked up the jug of blueberry

syrup next to her plate. She poured some syrup onto her pancakes. Then she put the jug back in the center of the table. She let go of the jug, but it wouldn't let go of her. It was stuck to her hand! She shook and shook her hand, but she couldn't shake it free!

Beck looked at Fawn sideways.

"Okay," Fawn said, "that one I *do* remember."

Don't miss any of the magical
Disney Fairies chapter books!

Fira and the Full Moon

As Glory pulled back, the others leaned forward. The jar tipped over. The rest of the powder poured onto the cactus.

The plant shot up, knocking over jars and shelves. Its sharp spines scraped the walls. Fira grabbed the healing potion from the worktable just before a fast-growing spine knocked it over.

Fira flew toward the ceiling, trying to outrace the growing cactus. The cactus stretched toward her. The workshop shook with the force.

"I can't go any higher!" Fira cried when she reached the ceiling.

A Masterpiece for Bess

Bess closed the door behind Rosetta. She felt extremely flattered—and still a little stunned. It was part of her role as an art-talent to do paintings for her fellow fairies. Till that morning, they had always been for special occasions: an Arrival Day portrait, or a new painting for the Home Tree corridor. In between, she was as free as a bird to paint whatever she wanted.

But now, right out of the blue, *two* fairies wanted their pictures painted in one day! That was a record for any art-talent fairy, Bess was sure.

Bless my wings, she thought. *Who knew that Never fairies had such great taste!*

Prilla and the Butterfly Lie

An uncomfortable silence filled the tearoom. Some fairies studied their forks. Others examined their dinner plates very closely. No one would look up.

"No volunteers," said the queen. "This is indeed a problem. What are we to do?"

"I know!" said a voice. "There is a fairy who would be happy to help out. She *loves* butterflies."

The room began to buzz once more. Everyone wondered who the butterfly-loving fairy could be.

Prilla sank into her chair until her head was barely level with the table. She had completely forgotten about her butterfly lie.

Beck Beyond the Sea

Instead of trying to *imagine* the size of the world, why not see it for herself? Or at least, as much as she could see in a day.

She shouted, "Wait! Wait! I want to go with you." Beck leaped into the air, flying as fast as she could.

"Where are you going?" she heard Terence call. "Hey, what did they say?"

Beck didn't pause to answer. She couldn't. No time. The birds were already high in the air and yards away. She lowered her head into the wind and beat her wings as hard as she could. Faster . . . faster . . . faster . . .

Tink, North of Never Land

She'd been flying for a quarter of an hour when she looked down. Her heart sank. She was just crossing Havendish Stream.

At this rate, it will take me weeks to reach the Northern Shore! she thought.

But as luck would have it, the wind suddenly shifted in Tink's direction. She felt the carrier bumping against her heels.

Tink climbed into the basket. She let the wind speed her along. In no time, she had reached the edge of Pixie Hollow. Never Land's forest spread out below her like a great dark sea.

  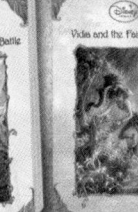 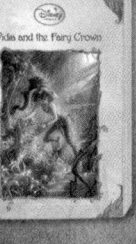